THE MAGIC
LAVATORY

Nicholas Allan

RED FOX

For Nick Bremer

Jeffrey lived with his house-proud Aunt Julia.

She was so house-proud that he wasn't allowed to play with toys, or friends, in case he damaged the furniture.

One day he opened up his great-great grandfather's cabinet. His great-great grandfather had been an inventor.

Inside he found a bottle of Thick Yellow Goo, and on the label it said '100% PURE MAGIC USE WITH CARE'.

Jeffrey poured the Goo into some cups and spoons. This is what happened:

Suddenly Aunt Julia came in . . .

She was so angry she snatched the bottle and poured all the Goo down the lavatory . . .

Then she sent Jeffrey straight to bed.

That night Jeffrey thought about the Thick Yellow Goo. Early next morning he was still thinking about it when, from the bathroom, he heard some noises; some gurgling, spluttering, bubbling noises.

Something strange was going on in there . . .

And it got stranger . . .

and stranger.

Jeffrey crept out
of bed just in
time to see
something creep
out of the
bathroom.

At first Jeffrey
was afraid, but
the 'something'
looked friendly.

It also looked
hungry.

Jeffrey gave it
some bread. But
it didn't like that,
so he gave it
some of Aunt
Julia's plates
which it did like
– *very* much.

It ate the cutlery,
and the kitchen
table, then
wandered round
the house
chomping and
chewing . . . .
A nibble here, a
nibble there . . . .

It ate:

A vase

A piano

A lampshade

A picture

A Persian carpet

A brooch

A chest-of-drawers

A sofa

Two armchairs

A Louis XIV
carriage clock

A washing machine

A hair dryer

A dishwasher

A potted plant

A colour television

and . . .

An aunt.

When the house was empty they did a little dance.
Jeffrey was *so* pleased with his new friend.

They chased each other . . .

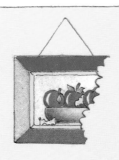

. . . and played basketball . . .

. . . and hide-and-seek.

After that they went out and scared people . . .

. . . which was great fun.

Finally they went to a railway station and caught a train. They had a wonderful ride all the way to the seaside.

Jeffrey's friend loved water and flushed with excitement when it saw the sea.

They went for a quick dip together.

TOILETS
THIS WAY

Afterwards, they lay in the sun to dry. Jeffrey bought an ice lolly and gave his companion the wrapper to eat.

Then he told some very rude jokes, which made his friend gurgle and splutter with watery laughter.

Towards the end of the afternoon they walked back to the station and caught the train. It had been a day to remember.

When they arrived home, Jeffrey's friend began to feel tired. Jeffrey realized the Yellow Goo was running out . . . .

Very slowly his friend started to change back into its old self.

Jeffrey was sad. Suddenly he felt very alone.

But just then an amazing thing happened.

Its mouth began to open.

And out stepped . . . Aunt Julia!

She seemed none the worse for wear. In fact she was so happy to be back and to see Jeffrey again she didn't care about the house any more – not even the Louis XIV carriage clock.

From then on Jeffrey and Aunt Julia lived happily together.

And Jeffrey was allowed to play whenever he liked!

THE END

A Red Fox Book

Published by Random House Children's Books
20 Vauxhall Bridge Road, London SW1V 2SA
A division of Random House UK Ltd.

London Melbourne Sydney Auckland
Johannesburg and agencies throughout the world

First published in Great Britain by
Hutchinson Children's Books 1990

Red Fox edition 1992
Reprinted 1993, 1994, 1998

Printed in Singapore

RANDOM HOUSE UK Limited Reg. No. 954009